Horse

MIDNIGHT

Champion Bucking Horse

Written and Illustrated by

SAM SAVITT

Of all the rodeo horses, famous and in-famous, Midnight was considered tops. Once his bucking career began, no rider managed to stay on his back for the ten seconds required to win. Yet there was nothing vicious about this stunning black horse. He simply competed with all human challengers, using his unique ingenuity to assure success. Midnight was admired by everyone, feared by some, and loved by a few.

This appealing story is told in the first person by the three men who knew Midnight best — Jim McNab, Vern Elliott and Pete Knight. Work-ing closely with Vern Elliott, the author-illustrator has recreated in con-versational prose and action-packed drawings a gripping portrait of one great horse and his exciting career.

A FOAL

MIDNIGHT

written and illustrated

NEW YORK

Champion Bucking Horse

by SAM SAVITT

PARENTS' MAGAZINE PRESS

Library of Congress Cataloging in Publication Data

Savitt, Sam.
    Midnight, champion bucking horse.

    SUMMARY: A fictionalized account of one of the
greatest rodeo bucking horses of all time told in first
person from the point of view of each of the three men
who knew him best.
    Reprint of the ed. published by Dutton, New York.
    1. Horses—Legends and stories.   [1. Horses—
Fiction.   2. Rodeos—Fiction]   I. Title.
[PZ10.3.S259Mi5]   [Fic]   74-5490
ISBN 0-8193-0745-9
ISBN 0-8193-0746-7 (lib. bdg.)

To William S. Orkin
my Father-In-Law

My sincerest thanks to Verne Elliot and the Rodeo Information Commission, Inc. for their kindness and cooperation in helping me keep the facts straight.

CONTENTS

INTRODUCTION

Ever since man discovered that he could slap a saddle on and ride him, or hitch him to a wagon and drive him, the horse has had a full-time job.

He has charged into battle to the din of clashing steel on steel, he has pulled caissons through torn battlefields. He has taken the stagecoach over seemingly impassable mountain trails, and carried the U. S. Mail. He has hobnobbed with all sorts of society and done all sorts of things. He has achieved moments of fame by winning a Kentucky Derby or a Grand National, or shared the spotlight with such famous movie cowboys as Autry or Rogers. But in spite of varied duties and changing roles, the horse has remained the servant, man the master. Most horses accept this.

There is one kind of horse that has reversed this scheme of things — the bucking bronco, rodeo's glorious misfit. His ancestry may combine the blood of ponderous Clydesdales and bony, snake-eyed Indian mustangs, neat little

Texas-bred cow ponies, and maybe a Shetland pony or a thoroughbred stallion thrown in for good measure. As a type he emerged late in the nineteenth century when farm horses were brought to the unfenced ranges of the West, and some strange mismatches were made, mostly at the discretion of the horses. The bucker's manners are very bad and his disposition is worse, and he doesn't go for this "horse is man's faithful servant" business. He believes man's place is on the ground, and has dedicated his life to keeping him there.

The rodeo world has known many outstanding buckers — Steamboat, Broken Box, Crying Squaw, Tumbleweed, Hell's Angel and the indomitable Midnight. Even today Midnight's broncy career is remembered as one of the greatest in rodeo history, and I feel it can be best portrayed through the eyes of the three men who knew him best; Jim McNab, Verne Elliot, and one of the top bronc riders of all time, Pete Knight. I am sure they would agree with me when I say, "There was a horse!" . . . And this is his story.

Part One

JIM McNAB'S STORY

Yes sir, I knew that Midnight horse from the
very beginning. Of course his name wasn't Midnight then, we just called him that big black
colt, and he came down from the hills one spring
with a bunch of other fuzzies all ready to be

made into a good working cow horse. He was a four-year-old, been saddle broke the summer before with the rest of his young buddies, and we had no reason to believe he wouldn't go straight to work with very few shenanigans. I'd been away to the war and was real anxious to get back in the saddle.

The gate of the corral was wide open and as the last one thundered through the opening, I swung it shut. 'Round and 'round they went with the dust so thick you could hardly see the hand in front of your face. They sure were a spooky bunch, been turned out all winter and I guess the unfenced freedom had gone to their heads. When they finally bunched at the far end of the corral and the atmosphere cleared a bit, I noticed this black one. And black he was, black as midnight, with a devil-may care look to go with it— and proud too. What a picture he made—head high, long black mane blowing wild, eyes flashing fire! I think what really caught my attention were his eyes—they were dark with that "look of eagles," and right then and there I got a hankering for him which I never got over.

"Okay boys, this one's mine!" My loop snaked out and when it settled around his powerful neck he stood perfectly still—waiting. I approached him hand over hand along the rope—

when I was about six feet away I stopped and looked him over. He was a well-made horse with maybe a strain of thoroughbred and a dash of Percheron, a little too long in the barrel, but put together real solid-like—stood about fifteen one and I figured about thirteen hundred pounds strong.

Seems like it only happened yesterday—it was a day like any other for that time of year, sunny with just the right amount of coolness in the air. I felt real good, no sense of foreboding, no nothing.

The saddle was cinched up—one of my boys had a good tight hold on his halter and I grinned and said, "Here goes nothing!" as I swung aboard. Now remember, so far this bronc hadn't made a wrong move—just stood there, steady, braced—later that was one of the things everyone remembered about Midnight—he never wasted energy—just waited until it was time. And the time had come, right now! I never

knew what hit me. Something slammed me from underneath — twisted my back sideways — jammed my face into the dirt, and then I was sitting on the ground looking up at him. This couldn't be true—no horse ever piled me that easily. Maybe I'd gotten a little rusty in the war, sorta lost my feel—"Hold him boys, let's try it again!"

Well . . . after the third try I just sat there on the ground awhile and thought things over. Hank, one of my ranch hands, cautiously joined me and we both sat there smoking cigarettes and watching the wrangler and his crew round up Midnight a fourth time—snag him with ropes from both sides, and jerk off saddle and halter.

"Looks like we got ourselves a bucking horse, boss," says Hank finally.

"Looks like," I grunted, "we've got the top bucking horse in the whole wide world—right now he knows more tricks, and packs more power, than any horse I ever rode. Man he's murder!"

Yes sir, that's the way it all began—on a nice spring day back in the year 1919—on my cotton-wood ranch in southern Alberta.

I had the reputation of being a pretty fair bronc buster and before long word got around that old Jim McNab had got his comeuppance —he'd been rolled in the dust by one black horse—three times in a row. From miles around ranch hands came, most of 'em to look and admire, a few to try their luck at riding the Midnight horse. Their luck was always rotten.

Up to this point I still couldn't get it through my noggin that Midnight would never make a working cow horse. I liked this bronc, I liked the way he moved, I liked his quick intelligent eye, and most of all I liked his heart. Here was a horse who would never say die—guess it was the thoroughbred in him. Here was a horse whose friendship was worth cultivating. I figured he needed a new beginning, a fresh start, and I proceeded to try to give it to him.

I spent long hours just standing out there in the corral talking to him—saying lots of sweet nothings—and finally I could run my hand over

his sleek neck and sort of pull his mane playful-
like. Sometimes I gently rubbed the velvet of
his warm muzzle, and when I scratched the
curlicue of hair on his forehead he would half
close his eyes in a sleepy way. And sometimes
I put my cheek against the side of his neck and
smelled the warm sweetness of him. It was sorta
like walking through a field of new mown hay
with a warm sun on your face. Before long, he
nickered and came to meet me when I went into

the pasture, then followed me around like a big black dog. He was a challenge to me but he was the kind of horse you couldn't rush into anything. I figured the slow easy way was the best way with Midnight—and now when I look back I believe I was right, because those were real happy days all filled with promise. As the months passed a strong bond of understanding grew between us.

One bright morning I slipped a bit into his mouth and he took it easier than I expected him to. I led him around the corral encouraging him with quiet words and soft cowboy ballads. We were getting there. Be gentle, be kind—it was bound to pay off. He looked a bit worried when I showed him a saddle, but after he smelled it very thoroughly and made sure it wasn't going to bite, he let me put it on his back. More walking—more talking—saddle off, saddle on—maybe three, four days of this. And then one afternoon I got on—after the saddle. He jigged

a bit and for one moment I thought, here he goes! But he settled down and walked out—and the day looked brighter.

Then came Twenty-one Johnson—you probably never heard of him. He was a shrewd one, that gent. Had himself calluses, too, from patting his own back. His racket was riding wild horses for a suitable wager and then investing his profits in sky-limit blackjack games. Johnson had a gimmick—he used a saddle with an eighteen inch swell—when he pressed his powerful thighs against that broad swell no horse alive could shake him loose. Anyway, that's what Twenty-one boasted—and he backed his claim with fifty dollars.

I recognized him one late afternoon when he was better than a mile off. You couldn't miss the dazzling white shirt, and nobody but Twenty-one Johnson displayed black sideburns that protruded about half a foot from each side of his face. I watched him drive through the front gate, long and lank, and all pretzeled up in the front seat of his buckboard with his saddle right behind him. "Hi-ya, Twenty-one—come to make a little money?"

28

He nodded, climbed down, hitched up his belt, and said, "Where's that Midnight horse?

His day has come!"—and maybe it had. The boys started gathering then—grinning, winking at each other.

Midnight was brought out, head high against a taut halter shank, lights jumping all over his sleek blackness, proud, defiant—yet almost casual.

Hank had him snubbed down while Twenty-one slid his saddle on, drew himself up and in.

"All set Johnson boy? Got those legs in close—good hold on that shank? Okay, Hank, let 'er rip!"

Down came Midnight's head and up went Midnight. So powerful, so urgent was his thrust that great clumps of sod followed him, and as he rolled at the top of his arc, his quarters twisted and shot skyward. Then the earth exploded and blurred and as Midnight came into focus again, I could see Johnson was still with him, but I could also see that he wasn't doing too well. He had blown both stirrups, had a strangle hold on his saddle horn, and his head was bobbing like a jack-in-the-box. They were going up for the third time now—Twenty-one's eyes were glazing fast—a big chunk of daylight leaped in between him and the saddle, and as Midnight dropped the curtain for the third time Johnson was on his way. Spread-eagled and spiraling out of the

sun, he slammed the ground with such impact that it took about twenty minutes and two buckets of water to make him realize that he had just lost himself fifty bucks—and his reputation.

After that slick exhibition I couldn't resist giving Midnight a whirl with the best riders in Canada. Little did I know then that I was launching one of the greatest bucking horses in rodeo history. I signed him up for the bucking horse events in the local stampede at McCleod. Two riders got him in the draw.

Rodeo rules require a rider to stay in the saddle ten seconds, using only one rein which cannot be knotted or wrapped around the wrist. He must ride with one hand in the air, and can't change hands on the rein. He must come out raking his spurs fore and aft. He is disqualified if thrown, if he pulls leather, that is, grabs the saddle horn, or if he "blows" a stirrup. Applying rosin to the seat of the pants is barred.

The first rider hit the airways in four seconds. The second man made a mistake. He gouged my black horse with his spurs—the first spurs Midnight had ever felt driven home in deadly earnest—and that was it! Before this it had been a game—you try to stay on, I try to buck you off—but when those spurs hit . . . WOW! He

squealed and twisted in the middle of a straight
buck, ears flat back, mouth wide open, nostrils
flaring red—you'd think he was some giant ser-
pent dragon from medieval times. The vicious-
ness, which up to now played beneath the
surface, burst outward. When his front feet
struck earth, up came that head, leaving the
man balanced against a flapping rein. As he
shot skyward again his rider followed the original
course—straight down!

Two seconds! That was all!—and the crowd
was on its feet! Here was a four-footed explosion,
here was a powerhouse with the disposition of a
buzz saw—an outlaw—a manhater. Here was a
horse to be reckoned with.

After the McCleod stampede we took Midnight back to the ranch. Hank went on up to the bunkhouse and I turned the black horse into the corral and stood leaning my elbows on the top rail, watching him move about the enclosure. There was an awful sinking feeling in the pit of my stomach. I had made a mistake. Even before I walked up to him I knew it was no use—that something between us was gone now. He backed off, watching me suspiciously. When I held out my hand and spoke, he snorted and wheeled making a half-circle to the far end of the corral where he stood, head high, with too much white showing in the eye. I knew then the damage had been done. There was no turning back, no second chance, and a great sadness came over me, an emptiness which left an ache in my throat that wouldn't swallow.

Well, several weeks went by or maybe months —I don't remember now, but I couldn't get that Midnight horse off my mind. I couldn't shake the depression that dogged me wherever I went or whatever I did. I guess I was becoming a little hard to live with and maybe a little hard to work for, too. I'd say to myself, "Jim, this is no way for a grown man to act. You can't let a

horse get you down like this—it's plumb foolishness. Now, buck up man, and forget it." But somehow I couldn't forget it.

Then a new situation came up which didn't help my disposition one bit. Some of the top riders from the big Red Deer outfit challenged me to enter Midnight in the Calgary Stampede —the biggest rodeo in Canada. They wanted a crack at my "wonder horse." I refused to accept their challenge, but when the Red Deer straw boss claimed I was afraid to risk my bucking horse against "good riders" I blew my stack.

Midnight was entered, and on the opening day of the Calgary Stampede I sat in the stands, miserable and remorseful, and cussing my wild Irish pride for being taken. A black premonition sat beside me—a strange kind of fright shook my insides and made my teeth chatter, for I felt that before this day was through I would lose my Midnight horse forever.

Red Deer's top bronc rider drew Midnight first. He settled into the saddle with grinning confidence. "Get in there real tight boy!"—

"Don't let him throw you now."—"Let's show that black devil who's boss!"

Midnight was steady as a rock, no fuss, no wasted motion. Chute number eight—the gate swung wide and for one breathless instant nothing happened. Then Midnight erupted into the light—a black tornado against a sunny sky, then smoking earthward with a whip-snapping shock that brought the blood spurting from his rider's nostrils. Three in a row like that and the man came clear—as if shot out of a gun into the earth. The roaring stands went silent in hushed horror, as Midnight turned and approached the unconscious rider. It's hard to say what a horse will do sometimes, and for one frightening moment I thought the worst was going to happen. Instead, he nuzzled the fallen rider, and as the pickup men broke from their trance and rushed toward the prostrate figure, Midnight carefully stepped over the man and trotted toward the exit. His job was done, there was no sense in rubbing it in. The stadium thundered with spontaneous applause—the spectators had just witnessed a top-rate performance. They knew they had seen a great bucking horse in action, and their hearts went out to him. Midnight had found his destiny in the swirling dust of the arena, and I realized then he was lost to me forever. I sat there with my head in my hands.

Yep, six days the Stampede lasted, and in that time Midnight blasted every man who tried to ride him. Each victory gave him more confidence, and by the time the rodeo wound up, he was going like a dynamo and getting better each time he came out. Upon his final victory he was proclaimed the champion bucking horse of Western Canada.

He came home in a blaze of glory, but I knew he was hopelessly beyond my reach. Seeing him every day at the ranch and knowing he would never be the cow horse I had hoped for was more than I could stand. So—I decided to sell him, never thought I could, but I did.

Animals have a funny way of sensing things. Somehow they seem to know what you're going to do before you do it. Maybe it's because we telegraph our feelings and thoughts in a hundred and one ways we are completely unaware of— I don't know. But I'm sure Midnight knew I had come to this decision. Out in the pasture he seemed to keep to himself and often I'd see him standing alone, his head high, testing the wind and a distant faraway look in his eye. Sometimes I walked out there, and now he'd let me come right up to him again and put my hand on his withers, my face against his neck, and he'd bring his head around and nicker softly. He knew we were coming to the end of the line and I wondered if in some way he felt the same yearning, the same regrets I did.

Calgary promoter Peter Welch became Midnight's proud new owner. He came for him on a cold wet afternoon, and I remember thinking, this day looks like I feel. There were several horses in the corral and as usual of late, Midnight was standing apart. He raised his head and watched me approach. When the others moved off he waited. He seemed resigned and a little sad, too. This was the parting of the ways. I think he understood, and at that moment a kinship arose between us which had been dead these many months. As I brought the halter up he dropped his head to meet it, and when I fastened the buckle I was looking into his warm dark eye and my vision blurred, and a cold chill shook my shoulders. I turned with the lead rope in my hand and he followed me out quietly. I couldn't look at him—there was a great weariness inside me, and then I handed the halter shank to Welch.

"Be good to him, Pete, he's a great one." I almost choked on the words. I turned away—my hands sunk deep in the pockets of my Mackinaw, my shoulders hunched against the raw wind. I heard Midnight go up the ramp—I heard the tail gate snap shut—the motor catch and accelerate, and as the van rattled down the drive part of me went with it. I turned then and I was standing alone. The world was gray and empty, like my heart.

Part Two

VERNE ELLIOT'S STORY

"We've got a humdinger bucking horse up here you ought to take a look at. His name is Midnight, and I don't think there is a man in the country who can stay with him ten seconds."

That was the essence of a note I received from Guy Weadick, impressario of the Calgary Stampede. This was around 1928—I am retired now, but at that time Ed McCarty and I produced rodeo shows. We supplied bucking horses, riders, Brahma steers, trick ropers, and most of the pep and vinegar for rodeos in the United States and Canada. I knew bucking horses—rode some pretty tough customers in my day, too. Maybe you've heard of the notorious old Steamboat. He was one of them, and a bunch of others— all gone now, because that was way back around 1910. I was a young fellow then, and in those days I absorbed a lot of punishment and a lot of knowledge—funny how those two always seem to go together. Anyway, when the old backbone couldn't take the beating any more I retired from active competition and put the knowledge to work in the game I knew best;

rodeo. Well, to get back to Midnight, getting a message like that wasn't very unusual. We got them all the time from all over the country. Somebody always had a bucker they wanted me to see—"Uncle John has a plow horse that nobody can ride"—"Joe's cousin Suzy's mustang took to pitching and there ain't a man alive who can top him." They were mostly false alarms, but once in a while you found something good and we were always in the market for something good. And let me tell you, the good ones were darn hard to find. You might ask what constitutes a "good one"—so let me put it this way: a good tough fighting bronco is likely to be born, not made. The meaner and more murderous he is, the higher the esteem in which he is held by the cowboy who rides him, the stock contractor who owns him, and the audience that watches him battle his way around an arena. And above all he should be consistent—every time that chute gate swings open he should come out fighting, and never say die! That kind is difficult to come by. I remember chasing down one of these prospects—sent two of my top boys to try him out. "He's got what it takes," they both reported, and I promptly bought him. Rodeo day came—chute gate swung out— and the son of a gun came out *running,* made two turns around the arena before we could dab a loop on him. That little bronc never had a buck in him, and he never bucked again. As a matter of fact, he turned out to be a pretty good saddle horse! You figure it out. Shipping, change of environment, might do that to a horse. A new bronc joins the show—he's turned out with a bunch of strange horses and sometimes they gang up on him—almost like a kid moving into a new neighborhood, and if he doesn't have much heart to begin with he'll quickly lose what he has.

I figured this Midnight horse might be worth following up. Of course I'd heard about him, but like a good many horsemen I was inclined to be pessimistic. There was no question about it, he was highly overrated—but we'd see.

The day we were winding up the Pendleton

Show I corralled four of the greatest riders in the business. These men were Hugh Strickland, Paddy Ryan, Bob Askins and Bert Civits. Any one of them could stick to a bolt of greased lightning, and they were on their way to try their luck at the Winnipeg Roundup.

"There is a horse up there called Midnight," I said. "If he can dust any one of you, I'll buy him sure enough." And that's how I came to meet up with "Middy." A few weeks later I was gabbing with a couple of boys below deck at Madison Square Garden when lo and behold the "four horsemen" came slouching in. There were four sheepish grins when Hugh Strickland said, "Boss, looks like you just bought yourself a bucker. When that Midnight horse unhinges, he all but breaks a man apart. No sir, we never warmed his saddle long enough to spit twice!"

We paid two hundred and fifty dollars for Midnight and promptly insured him for five thousand. What's more, we bought five of his roommates to keep him company, and when they arrived for the Fort Worth Rodeo that win-

ter in '28, you'd have thought they were visiting royalty. The newspapers blazoned Midnight's fame, and our quarters had a steady flow of visitors and admirers. That was when I ran into Guy and Paul Wagner. They owned one of the biggest cattle spreads in Texas. I hadn't seen these boys in quite a spell, and we sat around reminiscing about the old days. As the conversation rolled from ranching into rodeos and bucking horses, Guy said, "What about this Midnight horse I've been hearing so much about—is he as good as he's cracked up to be?"

I still felt that Midnight was overrated. I hadn't thought much of the horse when I first saw him that afternoon—I knew that by the time summer rolled around the boys would be riding him into the ground, but I answered, "That Midnight horse is the best in the business!"

Guy was grinning then. "I've got cash money that says there's a boy on my ranch will make your Midnight look as if he learned his bucking on a merry-go-round."

My blood was up now—I figured I'd better put up or shut up, but I did one better. I met his bet and waived all rodeo rules except the time limit and "pulling leather." Word got around real quick that the Wagner oufit had a man who could ride my black terror.

That choice bit of information, plus the terrific newspaper build-up sure packed them in, and on the opening day of the Fort Worth show —there wasn't a vacant seat in the stadium. The bronc riding was the last event on the program. We always ran a show that way—it was like saving the best bite of cake for last.

When the loudspeaker announced the bronc riding, the arena became so charged you could feel the hair bristle on the back of your neck. Things would start popping any minute now— the crowd was on its toes—and finally—"Midnight, chute number 7!"

I can't recollect that rider's name now, but he was a big strapping kid—stood well over six feet with shoulders on him like a wrestler. Looked more like a bulldogger than a bronc rider, but you never can tell about those things.

Midnight was standing quietly in his chute— almost seemed like he was daydreaming—didn't look like he had a buck in him. You see, I didn't know much about this horse then—later I was to learn that this resigned patience was the kettle before the lid blew off. I think this sorta fooled the kid, too. He eased down into the saddle real cautious-like, but his face broke into a grin when the horse never moved a muscle. Now he found his stirrups, jerked his hat down another notch, and then he did something which I knew spelled curtains for Mr. Wagner's man. He leaned forward and got a real close hold on Midnight's halter shank. A bronc needs his head and neck to buck—that's where he gets a good part of his leverage. This rider's plan was to cramp Middy's buck, which is okay if you can get away with it. The rules of the bet required him to stay in the saddle for ten seconds, and how he accomplished this was his business—but as he was soon to find out, it was Midnight's business too!

Okay boys swing her wide! Here they come! The thoroughbred in Midnight gave him a lot of heart and a lot of drive, but his Percheron blood gave him a neck and shoulders you just couldn't manhandle. To buck, he had to come up in front and drop his head at the same time —and he did just that! The fact that a two hundred and fifty-pound man was anchored on the other end of the halter rein didn't mean a darn thing. When the gate swung open the rider came spinning out of the chute without his horse. He was a human rocket, and he hit that

ground an instant before the rocket launcher's front feet. I think that was one of the shortest rides on record. Midnight won our bet, but the crowd sure didn't get their money's worth that time. Guy Wagner figured he didn't either. "I can pick a rider right now who will tame your Midnight horse," he boasted. Ed McCarty and I bet three thousand bucks of the rodeo pool money that he couldn't. This time the rider Wagner picked was Pete Knight. Wagner offered him twenty-five hundred bucks if he stayed with Midnight for ten seconds. That sounds like a lot of cash for a ten second ride, doesn't it? But let me tell you—ten seconds on a horse like Midnight means having your backbone telescoped and twisted and jammed right through the top of your skull. It's like having thirteen hundred pounds fall on you with every jump, only it's coming from underneath. After it's all over you feel as if you've been run over by a tank, and every bone and every muscle in your body aches for weeks afterward. That's how come so many of these rodeo cowboys who've been at it awhile, walk as if they hurt all over. They do!

Pete was no yipee-kiyi-type cowboy. He was a quiet, even-tempered man. He was used to winning, and in my estimation he was one of the greatest bronc riders that ever lived. He had a lot of rhythm, and a lot of grace with a wonderful sense of timing to go with it. Up to this date he'd mastered some of the roughest, toughest broncs in the business. He knew Midnight was

not just the run-of-the-mill bucking horse. His reputation had preceeded him and Pete was not one to underestimate a top gun. He had twenty-five hundred bucks at stake and his own reputation to think about, besides. Midnight's quiet waiting didn't fool him one bit—and he slid down into the saddle with all the relaxed alertness of the athlete that he was. He was all set now—had an even hold on the halter shank with just enough slack to give him firm support and plenty of body freedom. The gate man caught his eye—Pete nodded okay, then the fun began! First time up and first time down and there was Pete still sticking right up out of the middle of him, and even though I stood to lose three thousand bucks, I couldn't help but yell, "Ride 'im Pete!" But my Midnight horse had other plans. Nobody was going to ride *him* today or any other day, and with that second jump he started proving it. One stirrup was flying free, and when Middy struck earth, Pete's neck snapped so hard I could almost feel the jolt right through me. Up and over again, followed by a vertical power dive. Things were winding up fast now—the cantle-board of the saddle came up from behind and caught Pete hard just above his hips and that was the end of it. Man and horse came apart real sudden-like—a clean break, and when the dust cleared, Pete was on

his knees spitting dirt and Midnight was trotting easily toward the exit. He stopped once and looked back, his shaggy forelock skewed over one eye. He seemed to be saying, "No hard feelings chum, it's all in a day's riding."

Yep, Pete lost himself twenty-five hundred bucks that day, but that wasn't the worst of it. He'd been tossed for it—but good, and it was a bitter pill to swallow. I knew Pete pretty well—he was always a good sport, and he was no different now, but there was a look in his eyes which I had never seen before. Middy had gotten under his skin—this horse was a real challenge. Pete had been given a positive dusting the like of which he hadn't experienced since he was a green kid, but he never said a word. That round was Midnight's, sure enough, but wait till the next time.

The next time didn't come for quite a while. Right now Midnight was on his way. We campaigned him from Calgary, Pendleton, and Cheyenne to Salt Lake City and Fort Worth and east to Madison Square Garden in New York. He was a smart son-of-a-gun, and as time went on he developed a technique that left a trail of broken bones and cracked egos.

Take Earl Thode of Belvedere, South Dakota. He was world champion bronc buster in 1927, 1931 and 1932. Four times he drew Midnight and four times he bit the dust in less than five seconds. There was a time when some people claimed this was all part of a big publicity stunt —the riders were paid to take a dive, but that was a lot of hokum. Any contestant would have sold his soul for the honor of being known as the man who rode the world's buckingest bronc— and that's the truth.

As you know, when a man fails to finish his ride he's disqualified—loses his entry fee plus a chance for any prize money, and many a rider who drew Midnight tried to swap him for a horse who would give him half a chance.

I recall one man who didn't have a chance, but he had a mighty good sense of humor. He was a third-rate bronc buster, who really had no business tackling Middy, but he drew him out of the hat and he figured there was no harm in trying. Like most of the boys in this rodeo game, he welcomed anything that'd test his skill and ability. If Midnight had come straight from hell, sporting horns and a forked tail, this lad would've grinned and bet his last buck that he could send him back to where he came from

with his tail between his legs. That was confidence for you, but it didn't do him a particle
of good, because with the first jump, he was on
his own and blazing his own trail through the
tanbark. That ride sure never made history, but
some of the boys are still chuckling about what

followed. Midnight was merrily bucking circles round the dazed rider—just for the heck of it. Suddenly for a moment he caught a hind leg in a swinging stirrup, and at that, the fallen gladiator yelled to a pickup man, "See that? I got off when I seen *he* wanted to get on!"

Yes sir, some rides have funny endings and some not so funny—but don't get me wrong—the rougher the ride, the better. No bronc buster can make a good showing on a horse that just cowhops around an arena, but this Midnight was satan on four legs. True enough, he held a terrible fascination for all, but you could hardly blame these boys for the way they felt. They had to make their living. And incidentally, the way the riders felt about Midnight was one of the factors that finally prompted us to take him out of competition—but that's getting ahead of our story.

Because such huge sums of money changed hands every time Midnight blew into an arena, before each contest we guarded him like the U. S. Mint. Only once did any fixer manage to get past that guard. As I recall, it happened in

Canada. Anyway, instead of exploding into the arena like a black tiger with a knot in his tail, Midnight staggered out of his chute and stood, head way down between wide-spread forelegs, and his quarters barely able to support him. Of course it was obvious that the man with the needle had been to see him. The judges declared no contest—the rider had to draw another horse

out of the hat, and Middy had one heck of a hangover. For about a week he moped around his stall, feeling real sorry for himself. Whenever I got the chance I went in to see how he was doing. I'd talk to him. "How's it going Middy, old boy? Feeling a little better today?" He'd slowly turn his head, and you could almost hear him say, "Not so good, Mr. Elliot—not so good." But he came out of it, and pretty soon he was ready to go to work again. Did I say *work?* Contrary to what many people think, a show bronc leads a darn good life. He's well fed and well cared for, and during the show season he "works" about six seconds a day, four times a week. Herding cattle seven or eight hours a day is for his

less fortunate brothers. When the rodeo season
is over the show bronc is turned out in green
pastures and bides his time until the next season
rolls around. That's the life that Midnight led,
only in his case he averaged *three* seconds a day.

Middy was a temperamental horse, and almost as hard to handle out of the arena as in.
I understand that Jim McNab was the only
man who really got to know and understand
him, but I think Mrs. Elliot was the only woman.
Many times when conditions were such that he

had to be exercised by hand, that is, led by a rider on a second horse, things would go along fine—if he happened to be going your way. But if he didn't—try to move a mountain sometime! Mrs. Elliot had a way with him—she always did have a way with horses, and before long she had that big black devil eating right out of her hand. Many's the time I'd see her riding along with Midnight on a lead line right behind her— head way up there and moving like a carriage horse. But that's as far as it went. Middy never once forgot who he was, and he'd never let you forget, either.

In the beginning when I first met him, as you recall, I was pretty certain he wouldn't last, but month after month and show after show proved how wrong I could be. You know, you never can tell about a bronc, or any other horse for that matter. Right now in some far off wheat field in Kansas there may be some big gentle hunk of farm horse pulling a plow—he's been working at it for years. Tomorrow he may explode sky high, and next week he'll be in the rodeo paying off the farmer's mortgage. On the

other hand the reverse happens too—real consistent bucker, been tossing them steadily, and
suddenly he's had it—comes trotting out of the
chute nice as you please, disappointing ten
thousand people who paid to get in.

But Midnight was an outlaw. To many an old
cattleman, a horse is an outlaw only if he attacks
a human, and such a horse is not allowed in the
arena. But by cowboy standards, an outlaw is a

horse that can't be broken, that refuses to tolerate a human on his back, and such a horse was Midnight. He showed no signs of letting up—he was an artist who loved his craft and worked at it with a vengeance. But let's not forget that many of the men who rode these broncs were artists, too. They too loved their craft, they too were dedicated, and I knew somewhere along the line, Midnight would meet his match. It might be Bobby Askins or Paddy Ryan or Floyd Stillings or a host of other top men. Maybe it would be Pete Knight—time would tell.

Pete's next time came at Pendleton, and his luck was just as rotten as it was before—as a matter of fact he didn't give my black demon as good a ride as he did his first try. I was standing by the exit as he limped out of the arena. "Take it easy, Pete," I said, "your luck's bound to change." But he just grinned and I saw that same burning look in his eyes—only this time it was more determined. "Two down for you Midnight, but this game's not over yet—not by a long shot." That was true enough, only the game was not a game any more. It was a battle

now, a struggle between man and beast. Both
were fighters, and neither knew how to quit.
They locked horns again at Columbus and Vancouver, and when the earth stopped rocking,
Midnight was still ahead and time was running
out.

In 1930 word was flashed from Pendleton Oregon that Fred Studnicka, an Oregon cowhand, had gone the limit on Midnight. I'll tell you the story of that ride. It may sound like sour grapes, but hear me out—then judge for yourself.

At Pendleton, local rules eliminated the customary starting chutes. A bronc was snubbed to the saddle horn of a hazer while the rider

mounted. In a chute Midnight quietly waited his turn, but he sure didn't go for this snubbing down business. He came out on the end of a halter shank all wall-eyed and fighting mad, with his ears so flat back he didn't look like he had any. Six men closed in to hold him down,

and when he reared up he took them all with him, and when he plunged backward they scattered like wood chips in a high wind. He gave those boys a rough time but they finally snubbed him down, and to make doubly sure they added a blindfold—the less he could see the less there'd be to get mad about. Maybe this was all very necessary, but what came next sure wasn't. Studnicka was all set, and as Midnight was freed the blindfold came off and was whipped hard across his eyes. In football they call it unnecessary roughness and in rodeo I guess you'd call it the same thing. Middy was so surprised he

78

went back on his haunches and sat there, and a good three seconds ticked off before he came out of it. And come out of it he did—like the mainspring on a watch when the holding plate is removed. He ripped wide open with a three punch combination that sent him in one direction and

Studnicka spinning in the other. The timing judge fired his pistol when he saw Studnicka sailing through the air. He called it a ten second ride but no one can convince me that it took Midnight ten seconds to make those three pitches. It was a "long count," and Ed and I publicly offered to bet ten thousand dollars that Studnicka couldn't stick to Middy under standard rodeo rules. The bet was never taken up and Midnight was still the undisputed champ.

Then came the third week in July, 1930, and the Cheyenne Rodeo. Until about twenty-five years ago all rodeos were held outdoors, usually during the summer. Today they go full blast all year' round, and such great shows as Denver, Fort Worth, and Madison Square Garden are held inside. However, no indoor show ever holds the glamor and sense of tradition which surrounds the big outdoor ones—and few, if any, appeal to the people of the United States as much as that Cheyenne shindig. Class A shows don't necessarily attract class A riders, but I've heard many of the top boys say that the one thing they want to do, before they hang up their spurs, is win in their event at "frontier days." It's great to win in any show, but the winners at Cheyenne become tradition. They say that Cheyenne separates the men from the boys and that's no word of a lie. It's the hall of fame of the rodeo world and like a great magnet it attracts the top riders and ropers and bulldoggers from all over the country. Yessir, the best in the business meet at Cheyenne and they're all in there trying. It's one of the greatest shows on earth, and that July in 1930, the thirty-fourth annual Cheyenne Rodeo was no different. Ed McCarty and I were there with our top bucking string—and of course Midnight.

Part Three

PETE KNIGHT'S STORY

In 1930 I'd been in the rodeo game maybe nine or ten years. Actually I'd been at it a heck of a lot longer than that, if you want to count all the years before I hit the big time.

I came into this world by way of Philadelphia, Pennsylvania—and that's a long way from a ranch near Crossfield, Alberta, where I was raised. Funny—that's the same part of the country that Midnight was raised in, too. I guess we both started our careers about the same time. He worked at tossing 'em, and I worked at riding 'em—so sooner or later we were bound to meet up.

Riding bucking horses was always in my blood. Even before I got out of grade school I used to earn extra cash by topping off the wild ones for the local ranches. There was nothing that whetted my appetite more than some rancher saying, "Pete, I've got a bunch that need straightening out—come on over and see what you can do."

And I always did.

I was pretty good at it then, but by the time I was fifteen with about two hundred broncs under my belt, I figured I was even better. You know how kids are—when you're fifteen you've got the whole world figured out, but by the time you're thirty you're not so sure.

That summer I tried my luck at a local show, paid my entrance fee, drew me a good tough bronc out of the hat, gave him a real good ride—and took second money, just like that. Pretty darn good for a fifteen-year-old kid. Ten seconds in the saddle, and he comes out with a pocket full of money and a head full of dreams you couldn't bust with a twenty-pound sledge. I was on my way! Of course the going wasn't as easy as it started out to be. I've got a lot of mended bones to prove that, but I did all right. By the time 1923 rolled around I was right in there—and getting better all the time.

I'm not a very talkative guy and as I tell you about myself and rodeo you might get the idea that I'm blowing my horn kinda loud. It's not like that at all. You see, to understand the finish of my story you've got to get a pretty good idea about the beginning. You've got to know what makes a guy like me tick and because there is no one else around to tell it—and because I want you to get things straight—I'm giving it to you that way.

Well—to get on with it—things were going along pretty good for me. In 1924 I split first and second money at the Calgary Stampede and from then on Lady Luck rode right with me. Sometimes there wasn't room aboard for both of us—but most of the time we were a pretty successful twosome.

My cash earnings were steadily increasing and I guess I won enough saddles and belt buckles to go into business. In 1930 I was headed for my first world's championship and I knocked off three more before I was through. I had plenty of ups and downs—and better than my share of glory, and it all added up to a lot of horses and a lot of punishment. Many's the morning following a tough ride, when I was so stove-up I could hardly get out of bed, with my head and neck and back feeling like they were one solid piece—and my kidneys all full of sharp pains and fire. Times like that I wondered if I were doing the right thing. I wondered if maybe I oughta quit while I was ahead—but it wasn't as easy as that. It was a way of life—it was an infection that got into the blood, and win or lose, you were stuck with it. I've heard people say, "It's a heckuva way to make a living," and maybe it is. And I've heard one bronc rider say, as he staggered out of an arena, "Man, a guy

can get killed around here!" and that's a fact, too. The money was small compensation for the beating we took—we paid our own transportation and our own hospital bills—insurance companies wouldn't touch us. We were here today and gone tomorrow, but even though some of us wouldn't admit it, we did it because we loved it. I say *we*, because most of the boys felt the same way. We loved the travel, and the new towns and the thrill of seeing them again season after season. We loved the roar of the crowds, the parades, the smell of horses— the challenge, the ride, the unexpected—the sun in the dust and the dust in our teeth. Sure, it was dangerous. On a wild horse you're matching what you've got against a brute that like as not wants to kill you. Sometimes he does.

But danger added spice and vinegar to living, so we enjoyed a full well-seasoned life. I figured one day I'd draw me a bronc with my number on it, but until I did, I'd enjoy what I had—and let tomorrow take care of itself.

Yessir, I'd done a lot of winning and the rougher the bronc the better I liked him, and the better I rode—any one of the boys will tell you that. If you ride him well, a good tough bucker will always put you in the prize money, and that was the kind I loved. I knew a great many of these broncs. We crossed trails steadily

year in and year out—and I got to know some of them real well. They were the subjects of many a bull session—and if you kept your ears open, you could pick up a lot of valuable information about riding them. "Smokey Joe fades away from the rein"—"Corkscrew bucks them off with his head." It was horse talk we all understood, but there was one black horse we all talked about that none of us understood. I'd never let a horse get under my skin but, by gosh, this one did. Four times that black son-of-a-gun plowed me under—and whenever I heard anyone mention Midnight, my heart jumped and I perked right up and listened and tried to remember what I heard.

There was a horse! And if you savvy cowboy lingo, you'll know what one rider meant when he said, "Midnight was the kind of horse you could go to the end of the trail for." Sure enough, he fixed my wagon in '28 and three more times after that—but me—I'm a firm believer that there ain't a horse alive that can't be ridden—and I was real determined to prove it.

I thought about him a lot—planning, figuring. Why, I remember one time, when I was laying over in a small town in South Dakota, I went to see a picture show— and in the newsreel, there was Midnight—big as life and right in there pitching. I stayed in that movie house till it closed for the night, and I saw that newsreel four times. I studied his action real close, but it's pretty easy to sit back and watch some poor guy getting his head snapped off, and know exactly what you'd do if you were up there. You can't plan your ride ahead of time, either, because remember, you're matching skills with the buckingest bronc in the business, and while you're working on one set of plans, he's working on another—and that's the end of that.

A wild horse will buck out of panic and desperation. But Midnight was not a wild horse— he was a spoiled one and smart, too. To watch him you'd think he was blowing his lid sky high, but that black hurricane was about as crazy as a fox. He knew what he was about from start to finish—and I did, too, for all the good it did me.

Along about the third jump he'd bog his head
down between his forelegs and kick the roof
off—and when he had you straining back against
the halter rein—his big black head shot up and
that halter rope became a rippling ribbon in
your hand, with just about as much support.
All this would happen much faster than I can
say it 'cause in the next particle of time, he

would highroll it for Heaven and when he came down you were left up there windmilling in mid-air. This was one pattern of bucking he did real good—but he had others, too—and combinations, all aimed at the same thing—getting rid of that man on top as soon as possible.

When Midnight came to Cheyenne that July in 1930, he had kept his record and his back clean. I watched him unload at the Union Pacific stock yards just outside of town. He came down the ramp, sleek and shiny—head up—still proud—still defiant— still unbeaten. And as he passed me little pinpricks ran up and down my arms. "One of these days Middy, my boy, just you wait and see!"

And "one of these days" came sooner than I expected—but I'll tell you about that when we come to it.

That Frontier Day Show was a lulu. It was old home week—sort of a reunion in Cheyenne. I hadn't met up with some of the boys in a whole year, and it felt real good to see familiar faces, and shake hands, and shoot the breeze. Bobby Askin was there—just in from Montana, and

Doff Aber from Wyoming and Bob Crosby from Kenna, New Mexico—and a whole slew of others from all over the United States and Canada. You hear tell about the quiet, soft-spoken cowboy, and most of the time that's true—but, by gosh, if you were there listening that first day, you'd swear we sounded like a cackling hen party. Mike Hastings from Wyoming, whom I hadn't seen in a heck of a long time, had gotten his leg broken in a show down in Joplin, Missouri. He had been laid up for almost a year and a half but he was all better now and all set to try his luck again with the bulls. Some of the boys had gotten married and their wives were with them, but the older married men usually traveled alone. Somebody had to stay home with the kids. I was still batching it myself. Footloose and fancy-free they called me, and I told everyone I liked it that way, but between the two of us, I just hadn't found a girl yet who'd have me.

Anyway—we were all feeling real happy, and real confident and mighty anxious for the fireworks to begin.

95

That first day there was a big parade right through the center of town. Music, banners flying, covered wagons drawn by yoked oxen, long-horned steers, Indians, fancy saddles and fancy shirts. I rode behind one of the bands with the clashing cymbals and rolling drums pounding right through me. Made me feel like the conquering hero going off to the wars, and I was all set to lick my weight in wildcats. The weather was with us, too—sunny and warm with a cooler breeze coming down out of the Rockies. It would make the going easier for both men and live-stock, and we were all raring to go. The show started right on schedule, and for five days everything went off without a hitch—with plenty of action, and the stadium jam-packed through it all.

Jake McClure from Lovington, New Mexico, won the calf roping. He was a darn good boy with a rope—but that pony of his—why he knew as much about roping as Jake did, and he proved it every time he broke into an arena. To watch that little bay horse slam on his brakes,

and take up the slack in a rope, was worth the
price of admission. Jake thought the world of
that little bronc, and wherever Jake went that
pony was sure to follow. Nothing was too good
for him and Jake used to say, "We're business
partners—I take good care of him and he takes
good care of me." And that was a fact, 'cause on
Saturday in the final contest Jake set a new
world's record when he trussed up his baby beef
in fifteen seconds flat! What a team!—and what
a pony!

One of the funniest horse and man and calf rhubarbs I'd seen in a heck of a long time happened in this event. I think you'd get a better all-over picture if I sharpened you up on enough calf roping rules to appreciate it.

The roper is working against time, but must not start before the starter's flag drops, and there is a ten-second penalty if he jumps the gun. The roper must make a catch that will hold the calf until he gets to him, but he's penalized if the calf is jerked off his feet in making the catch. He must throw the calf by hand, for if the calf has fallen down before he gets to him, he's gotta let him get to his feet and then drop him by hand again. He can cross tie any three feet, and when he's through, up go his hands—and that's it.

I can't remember the roper's name now, but he got off to a good start. Horse and calf broke into action at about the same time—his first cast was good, too—flying dismount—calf bawling at the end of the rope—pony back on his haunches taking up the slack—and then the fun began. That little critter was so full of beans, he

wasn't going to be thrown and tied by anybody. There they were—man and calf wrestling around in the middle of the arena. That pony kept a-backing to keep that rope tight, and that bellowing calf seemed like he'd grown three new sets of legs, all kicking at once. Suddenly, down they went in a tangled heap, with the dust so thick I couldn't tell who was on top. Then out of it comes the calf, running hard for home plate. He still had one end of the rope and the pony had the other end backing fast to keep the kinks out—but halfway down the middle came the cowboy, all trussed up real tight—dragging along on his face and cussing a blue streak. Man, I thought I'd die!

We were moving into the last day of the show now, Saturday July 26, 1930. I knew Midnight was in Cheyenne, but so far I hadn't seen him in action. Maybe he wasn't going sound and they'd decided to scratch him. I had heard he'd been having a little foot trouble, developed ringbone from a bruise. But that old Midnight horse had been at it since around 1919. This was 1930, and those legs had taken quite a pounding over the years. I figured he had every right in the world to run down. At one point Verne and Ed decided to have him shod, but it was like trying to slap a branding iron on a bolt of greased lightning—no go! I'd also read in the papers that some of the boys had protested against using Middy as a contest mount. They claimed it was unfair, since he was an unridable horse. The account in the newspaper went on to say how in 1929 Earl Thode had drawn Midnight at three different rodeos and had been eliminated each time. However, the Frontier Days committee pointed out an original and still-standing rule: "This show bars neither man nor horse. All entrants are expected to make a fearless cowboy ride on the mount drawn, and failure to do so means disqualification."

So far my luck was holding—but Earl Thode's ran out when he drew Midnight in the finals on Saturday. There was no wasted motion—in four seconds that old black warrior showed everyone he was still top gun. Maybe he wasn't as young as he used to be—but who was? And maybe his legs weren't what they used to be either, but a horse like Midnight didn't buck with his legs, he bucked with his heart—and that was as full of fight as it ever had been.

That was a day I won't forget in a hurry! In the finals I drew a good fighting bronc called Powder River Grey—rode him all the way, and when this event wound up, I found I was world's champion bronc buster. Bobby Askin riding Broken Box took second money, and Eddie Woods, the 1929 amateur bucking champ, rid-King Tut was bucked into third place. Eddie made one of the best rides of the show and the crowd picked him for a winner long before the final judgment was announced. In the semi-finals Doff Ober from Jelm, Wyoming, didn't show too well—everything he rode fizzed out, but in the finals he drew himself a real twister called Satan. Doff blew a stirrup, but not before that Satan horse jumped him into fourth money. Artie Orser of Billings, Montana, riding Invalid took fifth, and a broken arm to go with it.

One of Midnight's stablemates, Five Minutes to Midnight, was pretty hot that afternoon, too. The man who drew him called himself Canada

Kid, and that boy sat down twice in three seconds—once in the saddle and once in the dust outside the chutes. I'll bet he's still trying to figure out how that little ball of fire slipped out from under him so sudden-like.

Then they wanted to see me at rodeo headquarters, and when I got there they let me have it. "Pete, as a special added attraction we'd like you to ride Midnight—champion bronc buster versus champion bronc. One hundred bucks if you go ten seconds—how about it?" You know what my answer was.

From that moment on I was a different guy. Everything inside me jumped right to the surface—and when I walked out of there, I was a rifle with the front sight trained on one target— Midnight. I don't remember how I got there but next thing I knew I was standing down by the bucking horse corral. The sun was low in the west and the last rays were sloping across the backs of the feeding horses—making them all red and gold with the sky going dark behind them. My eyes ran quickly over the lot and stopped at Midnight. He was standing a

103

little apart from the rest. I circled the enclosure and got as close to him as I could—I leaned over the top rail and clucked. His head came up and those black ears shot forward and watched me—and there was no one else in the whole wide world—but me and Midnight. And I remembered Vancouver, and Fort Worth, and Columbus, and Pendleton and a whole string of happenings that went with them. And I wondered if he remembered, too.

"Hello, Midnight, you old son-of-a-gun." His dark eyes pinned me and held me and I felt sort of hypnotized and scared and happy all at the same time. "Today's the day, Middy—we're gonna lock horns again—only this time it's gonna be different. I'm gonna ride you, old friend, for ten whole seconds—and you'll know old Pete Knight's aboard—'cause I gotta hunch this is the last chance I'm gonna get!"

I was all sharp and eager now, marking time. My whole mind and body were keyed for just one thing—that Midnight ride, and nothing else seemed to matter.

Then it was time—the loud speakers began

spieling the news about the special added attraction. One of the boys yelled over, "Hey, Pete, time to mount up!" I climbed up on the chutes and crouched there waiting. There was a lot of hustle and bustle. I hooked one arm over a supporting beam and lit up a smoke, keeping my eyes glued on the arena entrance. Suddenly he was there—filling it—all thirteen hundred pounds of him and my insides jumped and came crowding right up into my chest. From the withers back he was covered by a flaming red sheet. There was a rider ahead leading him by a short halter shank. When the band struck up they started moving around the arena. The crowd was on its feet, and as he swung along a swelling roar followed him. His head was way up there with his long black mane blowing. He sure knew he was king of the mountain! He was approaching the chutes and I read the words against the red background of his sheet "Midnight, world's champion bucking horse."

He was below me now, uncovered. For a moment his back showed smooth and hard before somebody slapped a saddle on and began

cinching it up. This was all handled through the bars—a man would have been a fool to get down in that chute with him. Saddle was all set—"O.K., Pete, let's try it for size!" Off in the distance the announcer's voice boomed, "Out of chute number four, Pete Knight riding Midnight!"

I dropped my cigarette and heard it strike the ground. And suddenly I realized how still everything was. There had seemed to be a heck of a racket going on before, but things had begun to get quieter and quieter, and right now all that was left was the shuffling and the whispers and the squeaking of leather. I was in the saddle—I could smell him now and feel the heat of him against my legs. I pulled the rope rein up just tight enough, worked my feet ahead a little, and settled back some to sorta meet the first jolt. I caught the gate man's eye, and grinned, and my insides stopped rocking and slid into place. Confidence came running back through me like water through a damp sponge. Everything else fell away. We were alone—it was now or never —and as that gate started swinging out I felt his haunches go down and dig in and quiver— "We're comin' out!"

One second—

Two seconds—

Three seconds—

Four seconds—

Five seconds—

Six seconds—

Seven seconds—

O.K. Midnight, you win!

Well, that's about it. Pete Knight and Midnight never met again and nobody ever topped that seven second ride. Three years later at the Cheyenne show old Middy made his farewell appearance. Time waits for no man, and that goes for horses, too. Age was creeping up on the big black warrior, and he bowed out in an aureola of dust and glory by unloading two top-notch riders of that day, Bobby Askins and Turk Greenough. In 1934, in response to numerous requests, he was taken to England where he made his last public appearance in four exhibition rides in Wimbledon. When they got back home, Verne took him out to his ranch in Johnstown, Colorado and retired him to pasture. For two years he lived there with two other retired veterans and his endless memories of a glorious past. Nobody ever put a saddle on him again. But on November the fifth 1936—in the cold, gray light of morning—death quietly rode him out.

Word that the great old Midnight was dead found Pete Knight holed up for the winter on a ranch in southern Alberta. He never said a word, just got up from the supper table and walked to the window—and stood there a long time staring out at the blowing snow and the years that had rushed by too swiftly. All over the United States and Canada, the boys Middy had fought and beaten, stopped what they were doing and remembered, too.

And the following spring they bought him a monument befitting a champion and placed it over his grave. Colorado senator Chris Cusack wrote the epitaph, and if ever you're driving through that part of the country you might stop by and read it:

> Underneath this sod lies a great
>   bucking hoss
> There never lived a cowboy he
>   couldn't toss
> His name was Midnight his coat
>   black as coal
> If there's a hoss Heaven, Please, God
>   rest his soul.

Sam Savitt has been fascinated by horses since his boyhood in Wilkes-Barre, Pennsylvania. A graduate of Pratt Institute and the Art Students League in New York, he has written several books about horses and illustrated more than sixty, including Suzanne Wilding's popular *Big Jump for Robin,* now available again from Parents' Magazine Press. Mr. Savitt has won, among other honors, the Boys' Club of America Award for *Midnight* and a citation from the Junior Literary Guild for *Wild Horses Running.* He lives on a small farm in New York State with his wife and two children. His favorite pastime, when away from the drawing board, is riding through the Westchester countryside on one of his two thoroughbreds.